THE TOOTHBRUSH CIRCUS

Words and Pictures By
Alina Loux

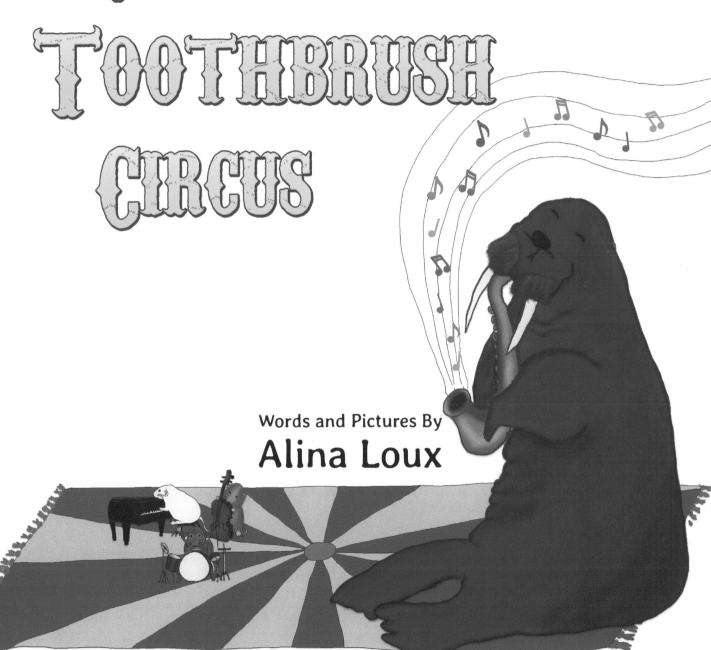

For Ember:
World's. Best. Kid.

For Adam:
World's. Best. Kid-at-heart.

Love you both forever.

Published in Madison, Wisconsin
ISBN: 979-8-9865279-1-8
Library of Congress Control Number: 2022913868

Edited by Sandy Ferguson Fuller, Alp Arts Co.

ken-ken books

THE TOOTHBRUSH

CIRCUS

Alina Loux

Shhhk-a-shhhk-a-shhhk.

Shhhk-a-shhhk-a-shhhk.

Do you hear that scrubbing noise?
Those **brush-brush shhhk-a-shhhk** sounds?
Look behind the curtain where a toothbrush world astounds!

Welcome to...

I am the circus leader. I perform for the crowd's delight.
But no! My toothbrush bristles broke! Can YOU help me out tonight?

First up, four fat walruses. Let's count their teeth... ONE! TWO!
Brush each tusk and feel the rush as you make your circus debut.

(Be sure you polish all eight!)

Up next, ten mustached, muscled men
to test your brushing skills...

What feats of strength!
What pearly whites!
What never-ending thrills!

Don't wait here in the spotlight,
put on your toothbrush show.
Shhhk-a-shhhk until they shine,
and look at how they glow.

Wow! Now it's the Mona Lisa, her smile a masterpiece.
Mon Chéri, if you please, touch up her petite teeth?

Pretend you hold a paintbrush, clean her palate with much care,
And floss between each tiny tooth, with such artistic flair.

Can you floss very gently? Clean her teeth with your brush?
FLOSS! FLOSS! GLOSS! Take your time. There is no rush.

Next, under the Big Top, dancing dogs need a cleaning,
Balancing on balls, twirling, whirling, swirling, leaning.

When you brush canines in circles, the trick you're bound to see
Is all their tails a-wagging, round and round in harmony.

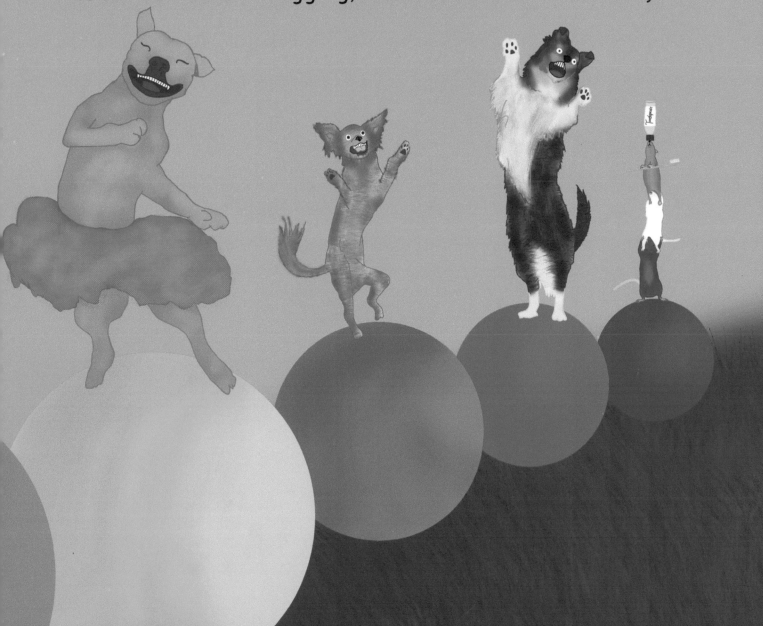

Beep beep! Here comes the big parade. First, a ferocious mouth...

A tiger in a clown car, with a toothalicious pout!

If you scrape the slime and grime away, he will not look so mean,
And polish up the clown car, too, let's get its grill real clean.

Look up for the finale...Who is shooting through the sky?
High-fiving and high-flying, the trapezist barrels by!
Human cannonballs need brushing, too, you'll have to finish fast,
She waves and dips...her brilliant face speeds by in a flash.

However can I thank you? You helped to brush them all.
Hooray! The crowd is beaming at the Big Top curtain call.

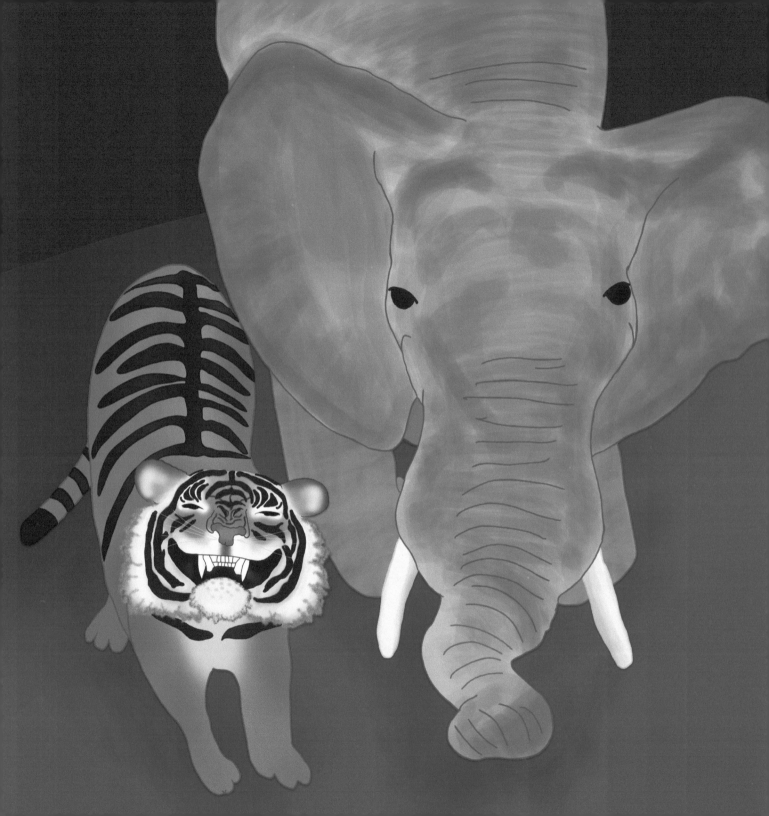

The Toothbrush Circus takes a bow, smiles gleaming in the light.

So...
Please visit us again... maybe tomorrow night?

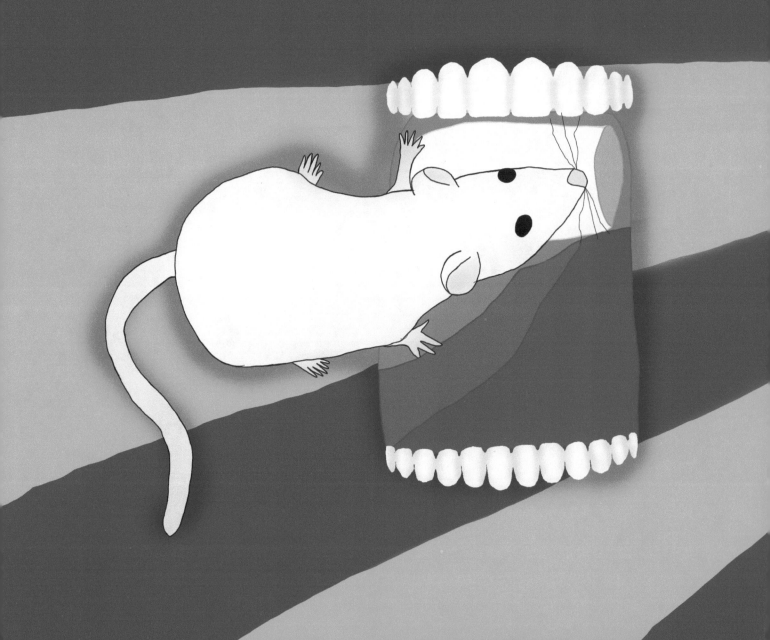

Shhhk-a-shhhk-a-shhhk.

BRUSH-BRUSH.

FLOSS.

CPSIA information can be obtained
at www.ICGtesting.com
Printed in the USA
BVHW021214020922
646135BV00009B/278